for John

\- J.P.

Summary: Join the Zairs as they learn sometimes our differences are our greatest gifts.
ISBN 978-0-9968263-0-3
Typography by Allen Gaoiran

# SQUARE ZAIR PAIR

**Written by Jase Peeples**
**Illustrations by Christine Knopp**

**In the magical land of Hanamandoo,**
**lived fantastic creatures always paired in twos.**
**They grew in fields of the purple plant patch**
**that laid spotted eggs from which they would hatch.**

They paired in two shapes, one round with one square
and the name of their tribe was the Mandoo Zair.
Once they had paired, their tails became one
joining the two in work, play, and fun.
Yes, one tail was shared by each Zair pair,
always in twos, one round with one square.

In huts they dwelled in the valley of Meez,
eating low fruit from the red berry trees.
The tribe lived in peace, or so I am told,
until a new pairing came to their fold.

**Two squares had joined and their tails became one.**
**Such a Zair pairing had never been done.**

**The others ran fast to see this square pair.**
**They flocked with heads cocked, they mocked and they stared.**
**"How can you two bond without a round half?"**
**They said as they giggled, pointed and laughed.**

"Away with you both. You'll poison our minds.
The true Mandoo Zairs are not like your kind."

Sad, the squares ran from the valley of Meez,
to a hilltop with two red berry trees.

There the square pair built a hut of their own,
where they could still see the village they'd known.
Like this they lived for six days and a night,
before they'd eaten all low fruit in sight.

**That's when they looked up, and let out a sigh.
There were more berries on branches up high.
Although climbing up first gave them a fright,
the square pair still tried with all of their might.**

**They found they could do what no Zairs had done.**
**They joined their square paws and climbed up as one.**
**Up high the berries were red, ripe and round,**
**much sweeter than those that were near the ground.**
**“These are most lovely,” one square said with glee.**
**“Yes,” said the other. “Quite nice, I agree.”**

"Let's bring a few down to our hilltop home.
Though it's a shame we will eat them alone."

Many weeks passed by, and though the squares thrived,
it wasn't long before winter arrived.
From angry dark clouds, fell great storms of snow,
that covered the hill and village below.

**The Zairs had never seen storms such as these,**
**storms that left piles of snow on the trees.**
**The low hanging berries all the Zairs ate,**
**fell flat on the ground from the snowfall's weight.**

The only berries untouched by the freeze,
were the ones at the tip top of the trees.
The Zairs in the village, though they did try,
couldn't quite reach those berries up high.

**Every Zair pair who began to climb**
**quickly came tumbling down in no time.**
**The Zairs became scared. Tears ran down their snout.**
**They stamped about, pouted, then finally cried out,**
**"What will we do?  There's no fruit left to eat!"**
**"Not one pair of Zairs can manage this feat!"**

**But the square pair, as they watched from up high**
**said, "We cannot let those hungry Zairs cry."**
**They ran down the hill as fast as they could,**
**quick to lend a hand, as friendly Zairs should.**

**They linked their square paws and climbed with much ease**
**to the tip top of those red berry trees.**

**They brought down berries for Zairs who had none,
'til all Zairs were fed, yes, every last one.**

**Then the oldest of all the Zair pairs,**
**approached the squares with the greatest care.**
**With heads held low, for they were ashamed,**
**they hugged the squares tightly, and then proclaimed,**
**"These two squares have pure and true Mandoo hearts,**
**but were mistreated and made to depart."**

**“Because they’re different we sent them away.
Yet it’s their difference that saved us today.”**

**“This pair of square Zairs knew what we should,
all happy pairs of Zairs are quite good.”**

**"Let's not forget what we've learned this day.**
**Each pair is special, yes, in their own way."**

**Then the whole village jumped and rejoiced.**
**Together they sang with united voice.**
**“From this day forth, we all do declare,**
**these square Zairs are a fine Mandoo pair.”**
**But that’s not the end, I’m happy to say,**
**‘cause something fabulous happened that day.**

**With their hearts now open, their minds had grown.**
**Soon each pair learned unique skills of their own.**
**Just like the squares who climbed the trees high,**
**another pair found they could leap to the sky.**

And a swim deep down to the ocean floor
was a breeze for one pair, instead of a chore.

Another could run with lightning speed,
while the eldest pair were the wisest indeed.
For each pair was special. Yes, it was true.
Just as they'd said, and now every Zair knew.